School Rules!

Robert Munsch

illustrated by
Dave Whamond

Scholastic Canada Ltd.
Toronto New York London Auckland Sydney
Mexico City New Delhi Hong Kong Buenos Aires

Scholastic Canada Ltd.
604 King Street West, Toronto, Ontario M5V 1E1, Canada

Scholastic Inc.
557 Broadway, New York, NY 10012, USA

Scholastic Australia Pty Limited
PO Box 579, Gosford, NSW 2250, Australia

Scholastic New Zealand Limited
Private Bag 94407, Botany, Manukau 2163, New Zealand

Scholastic Children's Books
Euston House, 24 Eversholt Street, London NW1 1DB, UK

www.scholastic.ca

These illustrations were done in a traditional crowquill pen, brush and ink,
followed by watercolour. Then the art was scanned and enhanced digitally.
The type is set in 19 point Charter.

Library and Archives Canada Cataloguing in Publication

Title: School rules! / Robert Munsch ; illustrated by Dave Whamond.
Names: Munsch, Robert N., 1945- author. | Whamond, Dave, illustrator.
Description: Published simultaneously in hardcover by North Winds Press.
Identifiers: Canadiana 20190175494 | ISBN 9781443182034 (softcover)
Classification: LCC PS8576.U575 S36 2020b | DDC jC813/.54,-dc23

7 6 5 4 3   Printed in Canada   114   20 21 22 23 24

For Cassandra Cautius,
Pickering, Ontario
— R.M.

For my daughter, Maria,
who reminds me of Cassandra
— D.W.

On Friday, when the bell rang and school was done, Cassandra hid underneath her desk and did not go home even when all the other kids got dressed and left.

She did not go home even after the teacher ran out to get to the bank before it closed.

Cassandra hid underneath her desk and did not go home when the janitor with the tattoos on his arms mopped the floor.

Cassandra hid underneath her desk and did not go home even when the slightly scary principal turned off all the lights and locked the front door.

Then Cassandra finally
got out from underneath her
desk, turned on the lights,
and pulled out all her
favourite stuff.

When it was time for dinner Cassandra's father said to her mother, "Where is Cassandra?"

"I don't know," said her mother. "I haven't seen her. I thought she was with you!"

So they ran around and yelled and screamed and hollered and called Cassandra's grandmother and all the neighbours. Then they called the police and the fire department and the hospital.

Finally Cassandra's father walked over to the school and saw the light on in her classroom. He banged on the window until Cassandra opened it. He yelled, "We thought you were lost! We thought you were kidnapped! What are you doing staying here in school?"

"I like school," said Cassandra.

"I don't care if you like it," said her father. "You can't stay at school. You have to come home sometime."

"But I like school!" said Cassandra.

"This is nuts," said her father. He jumped through the window, picked up Cassandra, and carried her home.

The next day was a Saturday.
Her father said, "You can't go to school."
Her mother said, "You can't go to school."
Cassandra said, "But I like school."
Her mother and father both yelled,

"You can't go to school.
THERE IS NO SCHOOL
TODAY!"

But Cassandra got on her bicycle
and rode over to the school anyway.
She knocked on the door but nobody
answered. She tried the window but
it was shut tight.

So Cassandra got back on her bicycle and rode down the street until she came to the Everything Store. She walked inside and said, "I want to buy a school."

"What sort of school?" said the lady behind the counter.

"I want a school with dirty red bricks, a slightly scary principal, a very nice teacher and a janitor with tattoos on his arm," said Cassandra.

"Oh," said the lady, "we have lots of those. Where do you want it sent?"

"Send it," said Cassandra, "to my backyard."

The next day was Sunday.

Cassandra's mother and father got up and went downstairs. They looked out the window and saw a school with dirty red bricks sitting in their backyard. There was a janitor out front cleaning the windows.

Her father looked at her mother and her mother looked at her father and they both yelled, "CASSANDRA!"

Cassandra came running downstairs and said, "My school! It came! This is wonderful!" She ran out the back door, said hi to the janitor, got scolded by the principal for being late, and went into the classroom with the nice teacher.

And at recess she told all of her friends how to buy a school of their own.